Clint Faraday Mysteries
#8
Omen

Clint looks at the very strange colors in the sunset. It is beautiful, in a weird sort of way – but those colors are just beyond his experience.

Silvio, a close Indio friend, says it is an omen. If the colors remain for one minute as they are, it is an omen of good fortune. If the pink intensifies to red, it is an omen of blood. Lots of blood.

Contents

About the author

CD Moulton has traveled extensively over much of the world both in the music business, where he was a rock guitarist, songwriter and arranger and in an import/export business. He has been everything from a bar owner to auto salvage (junkyard) manager, longshoreman to high steel worker, orchid grower to landscaper, tropical fish farmer to commercial fisherman. He started writing books in 1983 and has published more than 350 books as of January 1, 2023. His most popular books to date are about research with orchids, though much of his science fiction and fantasy work has proven popular. He wrote the CD Grimes, PI series, and the Det. Nick Storie series, Clint Faraday series, and many other works.

He now resides in Gualaca, Chiriqui, Panamá, where he writes books, plays music with friends, does research with orchids and medicinal plants. He has lately become involved in fighting for the rights of the indigenous people, who are among his closest friends, and in fighting the extreme corruption in the courts and police in Panamá.

He offers the free e-book, *Fading Paradise*, that explains what he has been through because of the corruption.

CD is the discoverer of the Chadam Protocol for curing cancer.

Facebook page Ambrosia peruviana for cancer.

Omen

<u>*Prologue*</u>

Clint Faraday, retired detective from the states, strolled along the beach near Cusapín. The town on a peninsula into the Caribbean in Panamá was nearby. He was in the comarca, visiting friends. He counted Indios as a majority of his friends. He loved the people and he loved their culture.

It was getting into the later afternoon. He was going to the mountaintop to watch the sunset with a couple of his friends. It was a special night, for some reason. One of the friends, Silvio, was a sort of medicine man for the people.

Clint didn't know – or much care – about the reasons this was a special night. He knew he was one of the very few non-Indios who were ever included in this kind of thing. He felt deeply about his acceptance by these people. Very deeply.

He had never felt the attractions and repulsions of people in the states, to a noticeable extent. Here, it was part of his life. He cared. He had learned to care his first couple of months in

Panamá. That was part of the major changes in his life. His cynicism about lifestyle and people in the states was unchanged. His acceptance of the lifestyle and culture of the Indios was fairly complete. It was an inclusive philosophy, where in the states and the Latinos and Blacks lived in an exclusive society – "exclusive" meaning "to exclude."

He realized there were some Indios as low and sleazy as many gringos and others he must deal with, day to day. His experience was that the Indios would go more than halfway in human relationships. They were almost never arrogant or judgmental of others. They made decisions and judgements about individuals, not groups.

Silvio and three young men from the town came out to meet him. They strolled along the beach for a few minutes, chatting. As the sun approached the mountaintop, Silvio said it was time. They headed to the road and got on horses. It would be dark down here while the sun was still bright on the mountaintop. It would be just at sunset when they reached the top.

This was the east side of the mountains. It was light here before the dawn broke on the west side of the mountains. It was dark a bit longer in the valleys than on the top, of course.

Clint felt the reverence of the people he was

with. They were not religious, in any real sense, and this was not about a god, of any sort. It was something that centuries of observing nature and cycles had taught them. It was not about, as many estrañeros believed, voodoo and magic. It was the nature of the earth telling them those things people who lived close to, among, nature needed to know. Conditions that indicated weather changes and such things in nature were shown plainly to the people who lived with that nature, not to those who fought it. The fighters had their science that was slowly revealing to them the secrets the people living with it had known since the beginnings of their evolution. It was a matter of knowing the language of nature and how to read and hear it.

Clint didn't really understand it. He accepted it.

They went silently, almost ceremoniously, to the trail and up the mountain.

The sun was just at the horizon, a huge blinding ball of silver light. There were clouds above and almost to where the sun shone so brightly, but there were none right on the horizon line. They watched as it sank below the horizon and the sky began to glow in strange colors. It was a bluish-white that quickly became pale pink, then more and more pink. The sky above and to the sides of where they were standing took on very strange aquamarine colors Clint had never seen.

Silvio shook his head. He said this was not good. Clint asked why.

"The color gets darker and there is too much green. There is far too much pink and it is not turning more purple. It is turning red. That is bad."

"How so?"

"Red means blood. Much red means much blood. It is not good! It must not be red in one minute. If it stays pink, things are normal, for that. If it becomes red, it is bad. If it gets very red, it is terrible.

"I do not like the green overhead. That is not

good. It tells me there is much confusion. It is not good, though it is not terrible. It is ... uncertain."

They watched for the minute, and a bit more. The sky stayed a darker pink, but there were a few blotches of intense red almost overhead, but toward the east and a bit south. Silvio discussed that with the others. Clint spoke the dialect, but didn't join the discussion of matters he didn't pretend to understand. He did catch that it was the uncertainty that was bothering them. It was because some few features needed interpretation. They were portents that only long experience gave indication of meaning.

Finally, Silvio said, "We do not know why there is red only there. We do not know why it is only small spots of red. Mario believes it means there is much serious trouble, but only for a few. Jorge believes it is a few here, because there is no red behind or ahead. It is not, most fortunately, over Cusapín. It is to the east. There is much jungle there and very few people. It is not something we can understand.

"I interpret the green and blue mix of colors over this place to mean the blood will not be here, but the trouble will be. In any interpretation, it is bad."

They watched the colors quickly fade to grey. The return to the beach was more silent than the ascent had been. Silvio refused to give an interpretation to the waiting people. He said it was not good for someone, but perhaps the signs were not for the people there in Cusapín, at that moment. It was very bad for people close to the east and south. It was a terrible omen for some, but he could not guess who. He could find no direct good in the signs. It was not directed in any way to Cusapín and the people there. It had connections, but no one could guess what those connections were.

A woman asked if the bad was to the gringo. Was he the one in danger of a bad omen.

"No. He was there with us. The signs of bad were to the south and east, not here. It is possible the connection here is *through* our good friend, Clint."

They accepted that. They were as fatalistic about it as about most things. The woman said she could not give a protective spell or amulet unless she knew what it was for. She said Clint must take very careful care. She was the local medicine/ witch woman. Her opinion was greatly respected. She was not feared, in any way, as in most cultures. She was sought for help, in a variety of situations. She was not known as an evil woman, but as a good one, what would be called a white witch in the US. The dark or evil witch was a negress on the edge of the comarca. That one was the reason of what little magic used was used. Counterspells.

Silvio had explained the system to Clint long ago. Their medicine woman knew that spells worked well if those involved believed. All that was necessary for countering most things was a belief as strong or stronger that she could counter the evil.

One could not counter poisons with spells. The dark witch was known to use many poisons and hallucinogens. They were very wary of anything from her or people who she used. She had no real power, on the comarca.

This left Clint with a lot of serious questions. Unfortunately, they were not questions that could be answered, here. He wasn't going to let it destroy his vacation among the people he loved. He didn't think there was any connection with him. He didn't know anyone south and east of Cusapín closer than the mouth of the canal, and few there. Apparently, that was a great distance farther than the signs indicated.

What was there? The coast, certainly, and miles and miles of rain forests. It was as much as uninhabited. A few Indios had fincas along the shore, but very few, and not close past the couple of miles with fast (relatively) access to Cusapín.

Silvio said the trouble could be as close as the farthest of those fincas, but he thought it was past them.

Clint knew that the omens were often based in logical happenings that had been observed over the ages, such as the red sky in morning one. That meant, in most places, that storms were just at the horizon to the east, the prevailing path of storms was from east to west, thus red sky meant heavy clouds to the east that would move toward you. Red sky at night meant the storms were already west of you, so weren't likely to affect you. He knew that a flash of green at sunset meant exceptionally good luck, in Florida. It seemed the local lore was that too much green was exactly the opposite. Science had shown that the green flash was due to the prism effect of clouds at a certain angle with a certain configuration. The earth is turning at a thousand miles per hour, so the prism band passes in a flash, to the observer.

Clint didn't believe the magical properties of omens, like the natives did, but didn't ignore them, for that reason. These people were right in far too many of their beliefs, for one reason or another. The red blotches didn't seem to him to have any basis, but that odd aquamarine color in the sky didn't make sense, either. The colors were from the overall prism effect from the angle the sunlight reflected off the clouds. That meant almost any primary color could show up – but aquamarine was far from a primary color. Scientifically, the clouds were curved in an odd way to make the effect longer than the flash to allow mixing of two bands – but blue and green?

He would worry about it some other time, if anything happened. Tonight was to be spent with his friends and was *not* going to be a downer!

The night was very pleasant. The group talked and told stories until after midnight, then Clint got a very good rest to meet the day. He was going to ride into the mountains on a horse with a bunch of friends. Some of them would drop out on the way to go to where they were working. A couple were going home, because they had stayed the night in Cusapín solely because he was there. He had helped any number of them, at one time or another, and was highly respected among them.

It was almost noon when he was high enough on the mountain that his cell phone could get a signal. Ralph Goins, a man from Manchester, England, now living in Puerto Armuelles, said he had been trying to reach Clint most of yesterday and into the night. Clint had turned his phone off in the afternoon so as not to be bothered by these people, who always wanted him to do them a "favor" that consisted of him wasting hours on some problem that they brought on themselves.

Sure enough! "Clint, I would really appreciate it if you could do something to locate some people who said they were going to that side to buy a large parcel of land where there's supposed to be some kind of mineral or something."

Everyone knew about that kind of scam. He had warned them, but they were insistent that it was a solid investment. They were so sure that he had sold them a big parcel just inland from Las Olivas, dirt cheap, with a part being in a sort of stock deal, where he would receive five percent. He would make a profit on the land he sold them, even though he sold it for about half what it could bring.

"So? What's the problem?"

"The, er, the check they gave me for the land bounced. I don't think they know their account was as much as raided. I checked, and the money was there, when I took the check, but was gone two days later, which is yesterday."

"What makes you think they don't know about it?"

"It was, uh, more that I'm a good judge of people, if I do say so, myself. They aren't the type to run a scam."

"If you could tell the type by looking at them or

talking to them, there wouldn't be any successful scams. I'm here in Cusapín, so can't do anything about it, anyway."

"I *know* you're in Cusapín, Clint! That's where they were going!"

"I'll be back in town tonight and can check to see if they ever got here. What are their names?"

"Ida and Harry Nesmith and Gina and John Littleton. They're middle-aged, but are traveling with a man called Frederico Valdez, and a woman named Guila Zacharia. Valdez is from Argentina. Zacharia is from Brazil."

"And the check, of course, was drawn on an Argentina bank?"

There was a long pause, then, "So it's a scam?"

"More than ninety percent."

"But ... but what do they gain? I simply won't allow the title transfer."

"At which time they'll make an agreement to pay, because they had no IDEA that the money wasn't there!" Clint said, dryly. "They'll then check with the bank and give you another check that you'll have to wait thirty more days on. It'll bounce higher than this one. Meanwhile, they use the fact that you're in business with them to work schemes on other gringos."

"I won't take another check from them. I'm glad you warned me. Is there anything I can do to stop them?"

"Uh-huh. Bad checks are illegal here. Put their asses in jail."

"I guess that's my only real recourse."

"You can run it back on them. Put them in jail until you have the money in your hands. If they actually have it, they can get it to you by direct transfer, not a check. If you get it, they won't have the backing to run the scheme against anybody else. You'll be a partner in some kind of scheme they plan to run here. There's no land not on the comarca between here and Colón, and not much in Colón."

"Then ... I don't get it."

"We can root out the bunch who're running the schemes. If they try some crooked deal here, it's the business of the Indigenos. They can handle the penalties."

There was a short pause, then, "And their ideas of justice are somewhat different than the corrupt courts here, eh?"

"It would seem so. Watch your back. I'll be in touch when I can get to a place like this, where there's a signal."

They soon broke it off. Clint looked thoughtful, then grinned. Maybe they could put the tails of a few of that type in a crack! He was willing to try.

It didn't seem the kind of thing the omen was

about, but who knew? If they were south and east and fairly close, it could be them. The part where they would be in serious trouble might be that they would have to face the charges in Puerto Armuelles or charges on the comarca. Maybe both.

They might buy their way out of the charges in Puerto Armuelles. They damned well couldn't buy their way out of charges on the comarca.

This might get interesting. Clint didn't see any way it could ruin his vacation or negatively affect his friends.

Okay. This was a scam, but who was it being run on? That the Argentinian and Brazillian were running it, Clint didn't doubt. What he didn't know was if the Nesmiths and Littletons were part of it, or if it was being run on them, as well as anyone else they could get involved.

He would wait awhile to see what developed. The only way it figured was a scheme to rope more gringos into it. Get them to invest cash, not barter, of any type. That meant money gringos – who would be damned wary of any deal that sounded too good to be true. Those things were what they sounded like.

How would they work it? The comarca land couldn't be sold. A person could get permission from the ruling council to use the land or enter it for a specific reason, but there could be no sale. It was Indio land, in general, and didn't have any individual owners. Simply because someone had a house and farm on the land didn't mean they owned anything. The culture was different. It would make it possible, even easy, to work a scam on people who didn't have a prayer of understanding it.

A lot of people came to Cusapín, for a variety of reasons, mostly for the clear water, beaches and surfing. Not a lot of them had much money. Clint still didn't see how anything would work.

He would think about it later. All he would do today was call Manolo, a friend/Interpol agent using a cover of a shady maybe-drug-middleman persona. Manolo could find out about Valdez and Zacharia as quickly as anyone.

He decided to spend the day riding into the mountains to places no white person had ever been – well, Dave. His weird friend was a botanist/orchid specialist who got along with the Indios as well as Clint. He came to these places with their blessings to do his private research and classification. Clint saw him spend days, and well into the night, pouring over pictures and matching them to notes when he returned from the trips.

He stopped at the few houses along the way to chat with friends and make new ones. It was a very pleasant time. He got back into town just at dusk, had a good meal and spent into the night talking with people. No one knew of any recent strangers from the states or Argentina or anywhere else. Dave had come there the day before and was wandering in the mountains, somewhere, according to reports. His ladyfriend was staying at

Elena's. He would come in at odd hours to unload his camera into his laptop, then be gone again. He would be there in the morning. Maybe Clint would like to go on an excursion with him. It was usually fun. When he was going and the guys didn't have anything to do, they would go along with him. He was 72 years old and they had a hard time keeping up with him.

It was a bit after eleven when he came in. Clint told him about the scam he suspected.

"I'm planning to walk the beach for about ten kilometers in the morning, down that way. I heard there were a couple of people here two or three weeks ago who were asking about the area down there. I'd like to see what's up."

"Want company? Maybe I'll tag along. Never know. Might find something."

"I damned well know I will! I found no less than nine varieties of orchids that aren't listed as being in Panamá! Three that are probably not listed anywhere! These are fairly close to where people've looked. Down there has probably never been explored by any botanist."

Clint listened to how he found the new species, but wouldn't file for names, if they actually were new species. He would let the kids (kids? They were in their twenties!) file through the comarca. They could name them after themselves or each other, their families, or whatever.

Clint got a good night's sleep. They would set out at five or five thirty. He had tried to keep up with Dave on a couple of the trips. He knew it was not a joke that the younger ones had trouble keeping the pace.

It was partly that he kept going off on tangents. The Indios knew that moving a bit more slowly meant you could go all day, but getting in a hurry meant you would tire yourself out, before long. Dave didn't tire out. He never slept more than four hours a night, normally. He had energy to spare. It was his body schedule. He ate more than most and worked it off. Clint did the same, to an extent. He ate a lot and moved a lot. He didn't put on weight. He could get it back off in a couple of days, when he started to get the spare tire bulge.

The dawn was beautiful, with a pinkish sky with silver streaks over the water. They set off with two Indio youths, who would tag along for a couple of hours or more. Andres and Moises. The parrots and monkeys were getting their noisy day started, too. They were both loud and funny. They would put on a show for the fun of it.

They were about two kilometers from Cusapín when they came to a little stream coming off the mountains. It was rocky and shallow, but the scrub and trees hanging over it were covered with orchids and bromelliads, anthuriums and any number of other epiphytes. Dave spent a couple of minutes, taking pictures of a couple of them. He explained that the yellow and brown one was an Oncidium that was only found in Brazil. He wasn't in the least surprised to find it there.

"No one ever looked for them here. Quite naturally, they didn't find them."

They moved on. Four hours later, they were eight kilometers (more or less) from Cusapín. They hadn't seen anyone for the last three kilometers. There were footprints going from where a boat had been drug onto the beach into the forest and back again. Moises said the prints were about two days old. There was nothing in the forest there but forest.

They looked around, then went on. Ten minutes later, they found another set of footprints. Clint noticed everything about the area where the others were found, and looked for something that would distinguish this spot. Nothing. The area was, basically, identical, with no noticeable, to him, features.

Ten minutes later, they found the third set. Andres said they went in normal and came out heavy. They were carrying something.

Clint and Moises went over the area inside the

forest, carefully, They didn't find anything definite. There was a small area where there might have been something.

"No pirate treasure, here," Clint said. "Maybe a drug pickup?" Moises looked thoughtful. He shrugged.

"If they found whatever they were after, there won't be anymore beachings," Moises pointed out. Clint nodded.

Dave found a lot more things that weren't "supposed" to be in Panamá. He would stay in this area and move slowly on and inward. Andres would stay with him, while Moises would go on with Clint. They found another set of prints, about half a kilometer farther along. There was nothing to distinguish the area that Clint could see. He asked Moises what was different about the spots, but he said they were the same, so far as he could tell, as everywhere else along there. "Maybe it is something that can be seen from the water, but not from the beach?"

That was an idea. Clint went to the edge of the water and looked back over what he could see. Nothing seemed different to him.

He shrugged. They went on down the beach. There was another spot, this one no more than a day old, about three quarters of a kilometer, farther along. Clint went into the water a short distance and said that there was a very tall tree back a short distance. Moises came out and studied it and said it was an old nispero.

Clint thought hard. He finally said he had noticed another one at the last place they found prints. It was directly back from the landing, as this one was. He knew nispero lived for thousands of years, so these could have been there a couple of hundred years as standout features. He had a case awhile back where pirate treasure was found by determining where runnels had been fifty to a hundred years ago. The Indios could tell very closely by the vegetation in the area.

"I wonder. Is there another map that uses a nispero as a loci?" he asked, of no one. Moises said there were probably dozens of maps that used nispero as a marker, but they identified land or such, usually. It was possible they were used to locate other things, but what things?

"Pirate treasure, I'd think."

"There isn't any pirate treasure along here. It would have been found years ago. A nispero wouldn't be used for that. Storms knock them down. No pirate would hide anything along these beaches, anyway. Someone could watch from two kilometers away and take it when they left."

"I know that, and you know that. Maybe some stupid gringo with a lot of money would *not* know that?"

Moises grinned, and said that was a distinct possibility. Gringos were ridiculously easy to trick, in that kind of way.

Clint gave him the finger. "How long ago were these prints made?" he asked.

Moises said maybe yesterday, maybe early today. Clint looked thoughtful, then said maybe he would go on a bit more. Maybe they would see something.

"They would be easy to see if they went on the water. That is exactly why there will be no pirate treasure. They are not far, if they are here."

Clint agreed. They would go a little farther, then back to where Dave was looking for orchids.

Ten minutes later, they came to an 18' Century with two 225 horse Yamaha engines, beached. No one seemed to be around. They went to the boat for a closer look, then followed the prints to a few meters inside the forest There was blood on the ground and shrubs. A lot of it. Moises studied it for a minute and said it was the kind of thing that bled a lot, but wasn't fatal – immediately.

"How can you tell?"

"There's a lot of blood, but no body."

Some things are ridiculously simple to figure. Clint could have done that!

"Of course, it may simply be that the body or

bodies – there's a lot of blood – were moved."

"Then there would have to be another beaching, close," Clint pointed out.

They went back to the beach and moved along a bit. Nothing. Moises shrugged when Clint said that meant very little.

"Very little? Why?"

"Maybe they didn't beach the boat. Maybe it was just a few meters offshore."

Moises agreed, with a nod. He said there would be blood in the sand, in that case, so they looked for it. They didn't find anything definite, but Moises said there was a place where it seemed water was poured onto the sand. That could have been to wash away blood.

Clint went back to search the Century. There wasn't much to find. They were about to head back to Dave and Andres when a man and woman came from the forest a short distance away to ask what Clint wanted in their boat.

Moises gave Clint a look and said, "It is not Mr. Faraday who wants to know why this boat is here on the comarca. This is Indigeno land in the comarca. I want to know what you are doing here. If it is something legitimate, you would have told us in Cusapín that you were here, and for what reason.

"I ask you, What are you doing on my land?"

"We're just looking for certain plants along the coast," the woman said, after the man translated. "We have permission from the government to go anywhere on national land."

"This is not national land. It is comarca. The government in Panamá City cannot tell you that you may come here," Moises said, sternly. "We have no objection, if people wish to study, but there are places here that are not to be entered by anyone not of the comarca – and few of the comarca. That is why we will insist that you make yourselves and your intentions known. We will tell you the places you may not enter.

"I will ask that you go to Cusapín to speak with the council before you again enter comarca land."

"We are on the beach. Everything to the high water line is public property!" she said, haughtily.

"No. It is not." Moises returned.

"The law says that everything is public to the high water line!" she snapped.

"True, in national territory," Clint said. "This isn't national territory. It's comarca. The law's different. You have to get permission from the council to be anywhere on this land."

"Like you did?" the man snarled.

"Mr. Faraday is with me. Isn't that rather extremely obvious?" from Moises. "I begin to wonder exactly which plants you seek. You have no plants. There are none in the boat. You carry no camera."

"Uh, we're with the medical association. We're looking for medicinal plants," the woman said. "I'm Doctora Elizabeth Channing. This is Doctor Carl Conrad."

"What medical association?" Clint asked.

"Er, uh, The World United Medical Research Project. United Nations," Conrad answered.

"Well, just go to Cusapín and talk with Obilio. I'm sure he'll say it's Okay for you to study plants," Clint said, quickly. "After all, we came out with Dr. Wullschlaegel and Dr. Dodson. He works with Dr. Maduro with medicinal plants, as I'm sure you know. And with Williams."

"Oh, yes! They did the major work with those, uh, Grobiarcanth plants, I believe?"

"More with Scaphyglottis, if I remember. I don't know much about the scientific names," Clint said.

"Oh, yes. I think you're right. Mendel did the work with, uh, the other," Conrad said. "We'll go to Cusapín for a permit, in the morning. We didn't know we needed one."

They said a few more words, then shoved the boat into the water and headed back toward Cusapín. Moises asked what that was about.

"I don't think there is anything like whatever she

said. Dave talked about Dodson and I made a ridiculous joke about an orchid called a Wullschlaegeliella Dave was studying. Maduro did a lot of work with Panamanian orchids. Williams was eighty or so years ago. He's been dead for twenty some-odd years. Anyone with a doctorate in botany would know about him, in Panamá. Dave has a list of more than a hundred species of Scaphyglottis orchids found in Panamá. He's found a few he thinks are new.

"I wonder if there's a body or two, back in there. There were certainly no cuts on either of those two."

Moises nodded and said he would have a search made, tomorrow. This would be in the area of the omen – and there was certainly blood!

"Blood, yes. But whose?" Clint asked. "I still don't have a clue as to what this is about."

"Or who is behind it," Moises agreed. "Or who those two really are."

"Who, indeed?" Clint said. They headed back to find Dave and Andres only a few meters from where they left them. Dave said he had pictures of no less than forty seven different species of orchids within an area of no more than 200 square meters of brush and rocks by that little stream. One might be a new species.

"Many Scaphyglottis?" Moises asked.

"Lord, yes! They're always all over this kind of place, here – and what in bloody hell do you know about Scaphyglottis?"

"I was talking with Dodson and Maduro about them. Scaphyglottis and Wullschlaegeliellas."

Dave gave Clint the finger. "Clint should have told you that Dodson's been dead a few decades. Maduro's out of Boquete. You might have talked to him.

"Did you find any pirate treasure?"

"No. Just some pirates," Moises said, seriously. "They claimed to be here studying medicinal plants."

"Maybe they were. There's a lot of that."

"No plants, no camera?"

"No camera?" Dave said. "Bullshit!"

"My sentiments, exactly," Clint agreed.

It was getting late enough that they would head back to Cusapín. Maybe they could find out what the hell was going on. It certainly wasn't about any medicinal plants. The very first thing any legitimate researcher would do was to talk with the medicine men and women in the area.

They discussed the two awhile, then Clint and Moises headed back toward Cusapín while Dave and Andres moved on along the beach a few hundred meters and went into the forest.

The so-called medicinal plant scientists hadn't

stopped in Cusapín. "They'll probably go back to where they left off, or a little farther along the beach. They won't expect us to be there," Clint mused. "Maybe I'll want to go out there in the morning – say half an hour before daylight?"

Moises grinned broadly and nodded. He made arrangements for Clint to be taken out about half an hour before daylight. They would look for the next tall nispero. Clint would be in the forest nearby to see what he could see.

Clint packed his Glock with his lunch and some coffee in a little backpack and had Kyle, a gringo friend who was there for the surf, to take him along the beach to about three quarters of a kilometer past where they found the beached boat. There was a tall nispero back a short way, and another a few hundred meters past that that was leaning at a noticeable angle. Kyle left him with a good luck wish and headed back. Clint went up the beach, carefully erasing his footprints with a leafy branch. He went into the lush forest far enough to be able to climb a small hill to where he could see the water, without being seen. He expected they would be there fairly early to be able to be away before the Indios could walk that far along the beach (which would be a serious underestimation of the Indios). Judging from how long that boat was in sight before they came out of the forest, he could figure they went to the nispero.

What could they be after? As Moises had said, there was zero chance there was anything like pirate treasure along this stretch for another hundred miles.

It was about forty minutes later when the Century came slowly along the beach, just out far enough to be sure there was enough water for the motor. Clint watched as they came along. There were two middle-aged people in the boat with the two from yesterday. He used the digital camera on zoom to get pictures of all of them. He would take more. The 2 gig card would hold more than a thousand pictures at highest resolution.

They came in to the beach, just below the big nispero, and drug the boat up the beach far enough to where it would stay. Clint was far enough away that he could only hear a snatch of conversation, now and then. They said something about Ida and Harry not coming back to the hotel. Valdez said they had seemed normal enough when they looked at the spot, yesterday afternoon. They didn't say anything about not coming out today, but maybe Ida was a little upset about something her daughter said when she called her yesterday morning.

After that, the bunch moved on into the forest toward the nispero. Clint wanted to know if maybe Ida and Harry's bodies were somewhere back near that last beaching. They were damned well not with Valdez and Zacharia when they headed back toward Cusapin yesterday!

Clint eased down and moved silently along toward the big tree. He knew how to move without being heard or seen in these forests. The Indios taught him a few things about that. He was near the tree in five or six minutes, but it took the other party almost half an hour to get there.

He came to a large boulder, not more than a hundred meters from the tree, and climbed carefully up to lay where he could see. The four were studying what looked like very old documents and trying to find something or other about twenty meters from the base. Zacharia said something about the rocks not being in the right places. There was definitely no bottle in a crevice in a rock. This wasn't the one.

They headed back toward the boat.

Clint slipped down and was near the boat when they got back to it. They moved very slowly, compared to Clint, so he was able to find a spot where he could hear everything when they got there. They came down onto the beach and were standing around drinking coffee from a thermos and talking about when the government papers would arrive. Zacharia said there was time. They wouldn't get in any hurry. Don't trust anyone who wanted a lot of money in a hurry. There were too many crooked schemes. Somebody who had to have that kind of money, fast, was probably up to no good. Get the money in a hurry and get out of the country with it in a bigger hurry. That was what she kept trying to tell Ida. Stop being so impatient and don't dump half a million dollars into the account before more was known. Get the accord, first, then worry about any money not needed for food or whatever. Valdez said he tried to tell her that, too. Harry insisted – but the money was going to sit right there until something was found. They would spend enough of it for gas and permits and such, and no more. What he and Guila had put in, already, would pay for all that. Don't get in a stupid hurry. Get the agreement from the government to explore and keep eighty percent of what they found before they put another centavo into it. If they found it now, before they had the accord, the government would allow them to keep maybe five percent.

"Do we have to let the government get involved in it?" the one Clint decided was John Littleton asked. "I don't see why we don't find it and get it out before they know anything about it! Why take half a slice when you can have the whole sandwich?"

"Because we could get stopped by the policia, like we did the other day," Zacharia said. "If we had one little item, the government would take it all and probably put our asses in jail for four years, on top of it. There's enough that even the five percent they would allow if we found it and reported it without permits would make it a good deal. Don't get greedy. You would end up losing everything. We'll operate strictly inside of the law and won't have to spend the rest of our lives running and hiding."

Valdez agreed, as did Gina. John seemed a bit miffed, but shut up. He then said he would have to transfer the money before the end of the month, or lose the fifteen percent deposit to the agent. That was his real hurry. Transfer it now, or lose double in fees. The damned banks were so crooked anymore that you couldn't even trust them not to try to screw you out of what you worked for all your life. It was purely sickening.

Yeah, and you're so honest and upright you want to find whatever and smuggle it out, Clint thought. He wondered if maybe Dear John didn't deserve to lose his ass. He might have walked away from it right there, if it wasn't for the suggestions about the Nesmiths.

"We would really prefer to wait until ... well, it will be safe enough in the account. Nesmith's half mil is there and our million. We get enough on the interest so we can operate," Zacharia said. "I really wish it was in your name, not ours. We could have worked out something. We could have formed a corporation."

"Uh-huh! And that damned lawyer said we had to move here and apply for permanent residence or something, which means we'd have to wait eight damned months before we even started!"

"It's been there almost two hundred years, so it won't go anywhere," Valdez said. "I don't like all this hurry-hurry."

"We have to hurry," Zacharia pointed out. "We were through this ten times, already."

"The damned lawyer said we couldn't wait or it would be two years before a corporation would hope to get permits. Getting them as tourists on a lark would be fast and easy," John said, acidly. "Even with this, we've had to wait 'way too long. Everything takes too long, here."

Clint could hear the Indio recognition call, "Oye! Oye!" just barely in the range of hearing. Back toward Cusapín. Moises had taken several people with him to explore where they found the blood yesterday. They probably found where the blood came from.

"What's that?" John asked.

"The Indios working in the mountains, calling across to each other when they pass. It's like 'Buenos dias' – sort of," Zacharia answered.

"It sounds like it's coming from the water," Gina said.

"They call when they pass in their cayucas. Somebody they know on the beach will yell, or they'll yell out to someone on a boat," Valdez explained. "We'd better get moving. I think we're very close. This is pretty well what was described."

"This is almost exactly what's there, but that was a long time ago," Zacharia replied. "I think today or tomorrow, we find it!"

"I think we should check that one up ahead that's fallen over on an angle," Valdez suggested. "It would have probably been straight up two hundred years ago."

"You're right!" John cried. "My god! What if the marker tree fell over, years ago?"

"Well, it could have happened, I suppose," Valdez answered. "I doubt it. Nisperos very rarely are affected by anything. That one back there is at least eight hundred years old. Maybe more than a thousand. They're tough.

"That's a good thing about them. If it's one that got blown down, or something, less than two hundred years ago, it'll still be there. Nispero doesn't rot and bugs and termites don't eat it. It's too hard. You can't even drive a nail into it. We'll just have to explore a bit more. We've already checked out seventeen of them in four days, so it would be inconvenient, but would only mean spending another week or so, looking, I think."

Clint heard a very faint call by the Indios to get the police. Valdez didn't seem to hear it and Zacharia had her head inside the boat to replace the thermos. Gina and John weren't supposed to know any Spanish, so only Valdez would have understood – so why the smirk from Gina to John? Why a smirk, not shock?

Valdez waved and they pushed the boat into the water and got in to head on toward the nispero on a slant. Clint waited until they were a good distance, then moved just inside the tree line for a couple of kilometers before getting on the beach to head for where he heard the calls.

Moises and four men were bringing the bodies of two middle-aged gringos onto the beach as he arrived.

"Well, Clint! Seems we found where the blood came from! Now we have to find out who they were," Moises greeted.

"Ida and Harry Nesmith," Clint replied. "We have to find what they were looking for, here, but I think it's pirate treasure. They have some old maps."

"With them?" Moises asked.

"Uh-huh."

"Could anyone be that gullible?"

"Apparently."

Moises laughed. "So they carry around paper maps a couple of hundred years old instead of scanning and copying them. They would be the ones who say Indios are stupid."

"Well, you are. You still can't catch up to the stupidity level of those idiots."

Moises grinned, and gave him the finger. "So we must know what, but we can guess."

"The 'what' I want to know is what bank these two put the five hundred grand in that ended them up dead," Clint corrected. "It's the twenty-sixth. The other two will end up dead before the end of the month, when their funds are deposited, I'd say. I'd also want to know what a certain look meant."

"You never make any sense," Moises accused.

The police boat came about ten minutes later. Clint told them what he knew, then got in the cayuca with the Indios and headed back toward Cusapín. He went directly to the computer and started looking up things. He called Goins and asked for some information, then told him Ida and Harry were no longer among the living.

"What was the deal?" Clint asked.

"Well ... I'm not sure."

"Find out everything you can about all of them. What bank, names in the account, who can or can't move funds, everything. Something is very wrong here. There's something that means ... there's a plot within a plot. Who's running what part?" Clint asked. "Ralph, I need that information. Today. Fast!"

Goins agreed. He said he'd call back within the hour.

Clint could find very little about any of them. He had their passport numbers from Goins, so could use his influence with the Policia Nacional to find a few things.

He went to the estacion to ask for information.

Salvador Esperanza, the head of the little police unit in Cusapín, got on the com to immigration to see what he could find.

"The Nesmiths arrived here on the sixth of last month. The Littletons arrived on the tenth. Zacharia and Valdez arrived on the tenth, also. I think they came with the Littletons, from San Jose', Costa Rica. They went to Chitre, then on to Puerto Armuelles. The Nesmiths were already in Armuelles, visiting the Wards, a gringo couple they listed on entry as friends from the same city in Kentucky," Sal said, ten minutes later. "I have business contacts looking for anything on any contracts. They opened a bank account, all of them, with a deposit of one quarter million dollars from Zacharia and Valdez and five hundred grand from the Nesmiths from cash transfers. The bank has a promissory from the bank of the Littletons for one half million that is to be deposited by transfer on or before the thirtieth of this month. Only Zacharia can draw funds, and she must have authorization from any two of the others."

"Have they applied for any permits or such?" Clint asked.

"Not with the government."

"You know something? I think this is two sets of crooks working two separate schemes against each other," Clint said. "Nesmiths probably thought it was legit. Muy interesante. Thanks, Sal. I owe you a beer."

"You owe me a couple of cases of beer. I like Corona."

Clint laughed, and left. He was feeling pretty good, so went to the local supplier and had two cases of Corona sent to Salvador's house. It would be fun to hear Sal try to explain to the gringo that it was a joke!

Next, back to the comps. He wished he knew which lawyer was supposed to be handling the permits, so called Goins, who said it was a local shyster friend of the Zacharia woman or something. Lic.Elena Sanchez Vargas Menendez.

"Is the money really in that account?" Clint asked. "I mean, the Valdez and Zacharia money."

"That's there, but is on a provisional deposit that can be withdrawn after forty five days. I checked."

So that scheme was running exactly normally. The others would put in their money, the account was in the name of Zacharia, but she could only draw with authorization by two others. Valdez and one of four people – two of whom were dead and out of it. When the other two disappeared, the money would be theirs.

What was the other scheme? Something still seemed out of kilter.

The Nesmiths and Littletons didn't know each other before meeting in Puerto Armuelles? That had to be checked.

Wait! If the Valdez-Zacharia couple were to disappear, was the deposit automatically withdrawn, or did it stay there?

A phone call, half an hour waiting and Goins said it stayed.

If it weren't for the fact the Nesmiths, who were probably innocent, were dead, Clint would like to sit back and let the rest of the drama play out. As it was, it might take some work to make things move away from either scheme.

Clint spent the rest of the day with friends. They went to the nearby river and up it a ways to fish awhile. When they came back to Cusapín, Dave and Andres were sorting through plants, putting numbered tags on them, and planting them in the trees around the house. Andres had about a hectare of land he was using, with plenty of trees, so they were making a botanical garden there, with as many of the local species of orchids, bromeliads, rhipsalis, anthuriums – and any other special types of epiphytic plants. Dave said the Century went by twice while he was where he could see the water, toward Cusapín, just past noon, and back again, about an hour and a half later. The women weren't aboard when they went out the second time.

They weren't staying in Cusapín. Where were they?

It had to be Chiriqui Grande. That fast a boat could make Chiriqui in half an hour. Half an hour for food or whatever, then return.

Clint asked if there was a boat to Chiriqui Grande that late. Moises said he would take him and spend the night in Chiriqui Grande. They could make it just a little after dark.

That may be good. If anyone was watching for him to go back to Chiriqui Grande, they would probably not be watching after dark. Dave said he'd keep an eye out for anytime they moved. Nicanor was on the dock, watching for the boat to return. It would stop for fuel, probably.

"They refuel here?" Clint asked.

"Yes."

Clint considered. If they went all the way to Chiriqui Grande, they would buy fuel there. It was a dollar a gallon cheaper. Something was strange about that, too.

The trip to Chiriqui Grande was interesting, in that Clint checked everywhere along the way where the Century could have landed close to a house or small settlement. There were several areas, but nothing definite. They were getting close to Chiriqui Grande when Clint saw the

Century back just at a distance where it could be noted, mainly because it was dusk and it had on running lights. He watched as it went to shore about two kilometers before where they were. Five kilometers from Chiriqui Grande, more or less. There were a couple of small houses along there, but no evidence the Century had been to them.

So. They were camping, somewhere out of sight. The morning might just be fun!

Clint had Moises take him along just out from the beach until he could see the Century pulled up between some large boulders near where a stream came into the Caribbean. He went ashore and Moises would go on toward Cusapín like normal and would wait a kilometer farther along.

Clint went close to the shrubbery until he was about a hundred meters from the boat, then went inside the shrubbery to the base of the hill. He would have to go around away from the beach to not be seen. It was slow, but he found the two large tents in a depression between two hills, where a small stream flowed into the larger one, two hundred meters from the Caribbean. The women were by a small kerosene stove, cooking something for breakfast. Clint moved to where he could hear. There was plenty of cover to within ten feet of the tents. The stove was between, with a small frond cover built over it. There was coffee on the stove and eggs and salchichas were on the second burner.

"... maybe too close. I didn't like him, and said so, then they got smart, but Rondo came and they left.

"I don't like Panama City, even a little bit," Zacharia was saying.

"I know. I don't, either," Gina replied, "I do like Puerto Armuelles, though. ...."

They went on for about ten minutes, with normal chatter. Valdez came out and poured coffee, then John joined them. They chatted about various inconsequentialities for awhile, then took some things from the tents to the boat. They said they'd drop Gina and Harry off in Chiriqui Grande, then go back to search around the tree where they found the bottle in the rocks. It looked very much like what was on the map. They would come back at two to pick up the Littletons and return to the search, if they hadn't found it.

So. The Littletons were going to be gone for the morning.

"Can you be back by two?" Zacharia asked.

"We'll take the bus to David. It's almost empty this early, then we can grab a taxi, if the bus is full. It won't take more than half an hour at the bank," John promised. "We'll be here at two! I hope you'll be here with pictures of the find!"

They laughed and joked a bit, then got in the Century to head for Chiriqui Grande. Clint went out, when they were finally out of sight, to check over the tents, but there was nothing out of the ordinary, there. He called Salvator, in Chiriqui Grande, and asked that he get on the bus with the Littletons and see where they go. He went along the beach to Moises. They waited for the Century to go by, but it didn't come.

"You know something?" Clint mused. "I think maybe the funds are supposed to be transferred today. Zacharia and Valdez aren't going to go after some treasure they know damned well isn't there. They're probably in Chiriqui Grande."

Moises nodded. They headed for Chiriqui Grande. When they got to the docks, Moises said he'd try to find where the Valdez and Zacharia people were. Clint would go to the bombas and check on the Littletons. He decided to try to call Salvator, though the bus would be in the mountains, by now, so there wasn't much chance he'd get reception.

Salvador answered, almost immediately. He said they were in Mali.

"You only got that far? You should be twenty kilometers into the mountains by now!"

"They got out here. They're waiting for the next bus back. About fifteen minutes."

"Were Valdez and Zacharia there when they got on the bus?"

"Uh-huh."

"Don't catch the same bus they do, back. It would be too suspicious."

"I know. I'll call when they get on the bus."

"I can be here to yell 'Surprise!' at them."

Salvator laughed. Eight minutes later, Salvator called to say they just got on the bus. Clint waited at the bombas restaurante until the bus arrived and the Littletons got off. Clint followed them as they went into the restaurant for some snacks and coffee. Moises called to say his subjects went to Punta Robalo.

That would be logical. They would have to come into the dock at two to act like they were just coming from "The Find" Clint was sure they would announce. They would go to their treasure – but wouldn't come back.

Or Valdez and Zacharia wouldn't come back.

Or something.

Clint had a snack, and sat, not far from his subjects. He couldn't hear much, but they seemed to have a rather intense conversation. Gina was pretty obviously giving orders. She would lean close and have a very stern look on her face, then sit back and look satisfied.

John got up, after awhile, checked his watch, and bought some various fruit drinks in paper cartons. Gina checked them over and nodded, then took part of them into the restroom with her, was gone about ten minutes, came back, and they paid the cuenta and went out to hail a taxi.

Clint shook his head. He wondered what would happen to anyone who had the great misfortune to drink any of those juices she took into the restroom.

Clint took a taxi, soon, and followed them at a distance to the dock, where they sat at a table to the side and had coffee and hojaldres. They were there at two thirty five, when the Century came from the east to the dock. Valdez and Zacharia were dirty and disheveled (Clint loved that word!). Zacharia help up a camera and gave the "V" sign.

Uh-huh! Clint looked back at the direction they supposedly came from and grinned. This might be fun! The two in the Century didn't know much about the weather patterns here, it was plain!

<u>*The Thot Plickens*</u>

Sometimes, the best laid schemes of thugs and thieves go awry. The Century came to the dock. The four went to the table Gina and John had occupied for the past half hour. Zacharia showed Gina and John pictures in the digital camera. They discussed them for a few minutes. They were calling for the cuenta when there was a sharp crack of thunder from the heavy clouds to the southeast, and the wind suddenly began to pick up. There was no way a sane person would go out into that. It wouldn't last long, but would be pretty intense. Valdez looked back and shook his head. Zacharia looked like she was about to explode. Gina gave John a sharp, hard look. John shrugged, and rolled his eyes.

Clint giggled to himself. This would be nervewracking for all of them. Clint estimated the little storm would last from forty-five minutes to an hour.

Clint also wondered how Valdez and Zacharia would explain how they came from where that storm was to Chiriqui Grande and didn't seem aware of it when they landed. It was between

Chiriqui Grande and Cusapín. If they came from east of Cusapín within the past two hours or more, they had to go through it.

The four went to the boat to get the weather report. It said the storm would be strong locally and would pass Chiriqui Grande in an hour and a half. Small and pleasure boaters were warned to get to safe port until it passed.

Gina put the juices in the cooler. Zacharia started to take one, but John said they would go to the restaurant to wait out the little storm, so shouldn't decrease their stores. They didn't know how long it would take to dig it up. If it was long, they might need them. They would have to do some physical labor – as Valdez and Zacharia certainly knew!

They went to the restaurant across the street and sat chattering at each other. The storm lasted almost two hours, when it arrived, forty minutes later.

Gina said they had better go to the camp and wait until morning to start digging. Valdez agreed. They got into the boat and headed out. When they were gone for twenty minutes, Clint had Eladio, a friend from Bocas Town, take him on his fast boat to Cusapín. He had an idea things might get a bit testy before morning. Maybe none of them would be around, by then.

Clint called Goins to see what was happening in Puerto Armuelles. Goins said he had secured the money in the bank. He could show he was owed almost half of it for the land he sold them on contingency. If they tried to abscond with the funds, they were in for a real surprise! He seemed very self-satisfied, to Clint.

Clint called Judi Lum, his attractive neighbor, who helped with a lot of his cases. She was very expert about collecting odd information from an unexpected angle. She said she would find out what she could. Who needed investigating?

"Ralph Goins, Puerto Armuelles. And find out which lawyers he uses. Something is very strange about this mess," Clint answered.

"Dave came in with umpty-dozen new orchids. They're hanging all over my place and his. Even Ben has some for him," she replied. "He said you were in some kind of weird situation in Cusapín and along the coast. Two people were already dead. Some people told you they were looking for medicinal plants, but ... Clint?"

Clint had let out a snort. Why didn't any of them react when they learned the Nesmiths were no longer among the living?

Because everything is exactly according to plan, stupid! That meant the Littletons knew their great buddies and partners would kill off those two.

That meant they knew damned well they were to be next – unless they made those great buddies the next two. This could get very interesting. Clint wondered who was manipulating whom.

He got a silly grin on his face. "It won't work, pal!" he exclaimed.

"What won't work?" Judi asked.

"A scheme within a scheme within a scheme. I wonder if that's the whole thing?"

"You never make any damned sense!"

"Nothing about this does, unless you look at it from.... I don't know if this is fun or scary or just so screwed up.... I'll know more, by morning – but will it be enough?

"Judi, there's a person involved in this no one suspects. I think I know who."

"I won't even ask what you're blabbing about."

"I wonder. Do any of them have a clue?"

"About what?"

"About anything, at all. I think we're in the middle of a bunch of crooked idiots! I really do!"

Judi knew he wouldn't make any sense. He had figured what was going on and how to counter it, or something. She would learn about it when it was done.

They soon said their "Good lucks!" and hung up. Clint went to Andres' place and looked over the hundreds of orchids etc. Dave had planted there.

Andres said he couldn't believe it, but he was getting really interested in the things. He never had any idea there were so many different kinds. He had planted more than two hundred plants there – and no two were the same species! Some of the tiny bright flowers were amazingly beautiful when you magnified them!

He then went to the homes (Indios don't live in houses. They live in homes) of friends until nearly midnight, then went to bed. Tomorrow would prove interesting.

In the early morning, Moises took Clint to the Century. Clint called out, but there was no answer. He sighed and said for Moises to come with him to see if any of them were still alive.

Valdez was. Barely. Zacharia was dead, by the tent. Valdez was unconscious, near the fire. The Littletons were in their tent, him with his head split open and her from having her head almost severed with a machete.

"I wish I knew what poison she fed them," Clint complained. "I might even try to keep him alive to hear his explanation of this crap!"

He remembered the purse Gina had taken into the restroom in Chiriqui Grande, and looked for it. It was there. It had a syringe with about a third of a reddish-yellow liquid, still in the barrel. She had, apparently, injected the stuff into the juice cartons with the ultra-thin needle. That small a hole would seal itself almost entirely in those paper cartons.

Clint smelled it, but it wasn't cyanide and he knew it. It had a sweet smell, not unlike burnt maple syrup.

Moises smelled it and said he thought it was Sangria del Diablo. If Valdez lived, he would be a vegetable. It ate parts of the mind up. The Cuna Yala used it, some. He had no idea how Littleton got hold of any. They would never trust a gringo with it. Period!

Clint thought a minute, then suggested Moises report the finding of the bodies when he went to ask why those people were on the comarca without permission. In about two hours. Valdez wouldn't live that long, without attention. It was better he died than that he live in a vegetative state for others to take care of.

Moises agreed. He would come out tomorrow to ask what the strangers were doing there.

Clint found the maps and the camera. He took some correspondence in a locked case. A name he was beginning to suspect was in the case. Gina Littleton had the key in that purse where he found the syringe.

"Clint, take the poison," Moises requested. "I

think it was to appear that my people did this. The person or persons behind it do not know that the poison is not used here. It is from the Cuna."

Clint agreed. He took the syringe and a small bottle that seemed to be where she carried the stuff. He went through a lot of other things, but didn't find much.

When they were leaving, a small boy came from the forest and asked why all the gringos were dead.

"Because they were very evil," Moises replied. "They were trying to make it look like our people did this, but they knew not enough. It is better that you did not and do not know anything about them, except that they had a camp here. You do not know of anything past yesterday morning, because you have to work with the family. You have no time for these strange and evil people."

This was, of course, in the dialect. Clint spoke it fairly well, so knew what was said. The boy would be very careful to not let anyone except his family know anything about it. He would never say anything to anyone and would answer as Moises requested, if anyone ever asked him about them.

The boy said "Coin dega,"(Good morning) to Clint, and went up the beach and into the forest. Clint knew the home was somewhere close by, probably back from the beach half a kilometer and by the stream that came out here.

Clint and Moises searched a bit more in the area, went through the Century, very carefully, where Moises found some papers hidden under the console, along with an old .38 Police Special.

There was a permit with the pistol authorizing Conway Goins to carry it.

Interesting. Clint considered taking it, changed his mind, then said, "To hell with it! It could be important!" and took it.

They got into Moises' cayuca and went back to Cusapín.

Judi had called while he was out of range of the cellular. He called her to hear, "Clint, Goins is acting a little strange, according to Gena Castilas. He seems to be scared of something and is more or less in hiding. His lawyer is Elena Vargas. She thinks two people from Colombia or somewhere are using the same one – and that Goins didn't know that, until yesterday, when he got some kind of information from the bank about their account. She doesn't know what's going on. Vargas and Goins having the same lawyer in a deal with him and some gringos. None of them seemed to know about any others.

"Vargas is known to be corrupt as they come. Maybe she was doing the old Panamanian thing –

representing both sides in a case, where she comes out the only winner.

"Does that help?"

"If you only knew! It makes my suspect list turn upside down! Judi, I don't know what I'd do without you and Dave finding odd things for me.

"The whole bunch out here are dead, but you don't know anything about that until the police announce it, Okay? I'm not supposed to know, either."

"So you found the bodies? What happened? Somebody they were working a scam on found them?"

Clint laughed. "The schemes were with them working to screw each other out of a fortune. I'll tell you about it when I get back. It would be funny as hell, if the Nesmiths hadn't been offed."

"Which ones did that?" Judi asked. "I really don't have a clue about what you're saying, but it's fascinating!"

"They all did that, or manipulated the others into doing it. Now they only have ... I think I should go to Puerto Armuelles, all innocence and, `Oh! Gee whiz and golly-gosh! Look at what happened to all those lovely people! I really am wondering, why would anyone do such a terrible thing?!' or something."

"Clint, be careful!"

"*That* is something that doesn't need saying. Thanks, Judi."

They chatted a few minutes about their friends in Bocas, then said they'd keep in close touch. If anyone asked about anything at all to do with this, she would put on her airheaded bimbo act.

Clint couldn't suddenly go to Puerto Armuelles. He had to wait until Moises "found" the bodies and called him to report. He went to Basilio's place, where they talked about the world and how it had gone to hell, everywhere, except the comarcas. Clint turned in about one.

"Clint, I am here with Capitan Oliveros of the Policia Nacional," Moises said, when he called at a few minutes past ten in the morning. "It seems those gringos I told you about are all dead."

Clint knew the cellular was on speaker. He could here the background noise, so answered, "What does that have to do with you? They aren't in Chiriqui Grande?"

"No. They had a camp here on the comarca, maybe four kilometers from Cusapín. Two of them are dead and the policia can't find why. The other two were killed with a machete or hatchet or something."

Another voice came on then. "This is Thomas Oliveros. I worked with you a few months ago in

David, when those people from the Estados Unidas were trying to find the woman in Peru.

"Clint, this looks suspicious. It looks like the gringos people had poisoned the two Latinos and the Latinos killed them for it or ... that doesn't fit, because she would not have been in the tent.

"I agree with Moises. Someone else did it. They are trying to make it appear the indigenos killed them, or something. Moises tells me you may know something about it, because you were with him when he confronted them about taking things from the comarca without permiso. They told you they were doctors seeking new medicines, or something?"

"That's what they said, but they didn't know anything at all about medicinal plants. They didn't even have a camera with them. Two of them were murdered out there, three days ago. The Nesmith people."

"They were ... Moises, why didn't you tell me that?"

"You didn't ask. I didn't know it was that important."

Clint almost giggled out loud. Moises could pull that off. "Gee! I didn't think the fact two other gringos we saw with this bunch getting murdered a couple of days earlier in the same area was something to do, one with the other."

Oliveros sighed. "I can never figure what the indigenos consider to be important information. They have these little things that don't connect in their minds, for some reason."

"That kind of information won't connect, unless someone suggests it," Clint said, hiding the laughter in his voice behind a cough. "It isn't pertinent to life on the comarca. It seems to be something that happens to a lot of gringos. Such a sad lifestyle. Pass the patacones."

"I often wish I could be as basic as they are. They have a really enviable life."

They chatted a few minutes longer. Moises came back on to say he would be back later, if this policia thing didn't delay him. He had to tally all the coffee and cocoa being dried so they could take it to the market in Chiriqui Grande. His wife was out of rice and was giving him lectures about neglecting the home needs. Clint could picture the exasperation on Oliveros' face. Four murders. The one who found the bodies is worried about getting on the bad side of his wife for not bringing the rice on time!

They soon rang off. Clint now had a good excuse to go to Puerto Armuelles to consult with Goins about this strange set of events – and what the hell is it all about?

Clint got off the bus. He saw Goins standing in the doorway to a small local restaurant. He had called and said he was on the way. Goins was, obviously, trying to keep out of sight.

"Hi! Let's grab a beer. I've done nothing but ride buses all day," Clint greeted.

"Er, I have beer and some good stuff to snack on in my apartment," Goins replied. "I want to lay low until I find out what's going on.

"You just said all of them are dead? Even Valdez and company?

"I thought they were running the scam. Why would they be dead?"

"Everybody in this mess is running scams. All of them have backfired, except the top rung. You ain't it, much as you thought you were," Clint said, dryly.

Goins didn't deny it. He looked scared and sick. Clint walked with him to his apartment, where he had to go through three sets of locked doors to get into his apartment. Clint looked around the setup and shook his head.

"What?"

Clint gave Goins a look of pure pity. "You have all those locked doors and bars – except for that big glass door onto your balcony?"

Goins looked shocked and mumbled that the balcony wasn't where anyone could get to it.

"Crap! I can come over that roof and drop onto it without even a security rope."

"I'd hear you on that zinc roof!"

"Not if you're not here when I come in." Clint inspected the door. He asked if Goins always left it unlocked, not that it made any difference.

"Never!"

"Then someone's already been through it since you last checked it," Clint warned. "You can get past the lock on these doors like this."

He locked the door catch, inserted the blade of his pocket knife under the door, and pried up. The whole side of the door raised about a quarter inch. Clint dropped it back and slid the door open.

"All you have to do is slide the stop over the lock, and you can't do that."

"God! I never thought about that! I just snap the lock shut!"

"Well, now that the horses are stolen, you can lock the barn. Got Balboa?"

Goins was shaky and pale. Clint was enjoying that. Goins got the beer from the 'fridge and poured himself a double Chivas Regal on the rocks. They sat at the kitchen table.

"What was here for someone to steal?" Clint asked. "Is it something they just have to know about, or something they would take?"

Goins got up and went into the bedroom. He stayed a couple of minutes and came back.

"Things have been moved. I left traps. They wanted a look at the account freeze information, I guess."

"Who's doing this to me! Why?"

"Licenciada Elena Vargas, because you're no longer necessary to the plan. You know what happens to anyone who becomes, shall we say, redundant. Exactly the way you set it up. You were being used the same way you used the Nesmiths and Littletons. You damned well know how that was handled long before you even got involved. If it weren't for the fact the Nesmiths were just two people who got suckered into it, and died as a result, I'd let her take care of you, then take her down. I still might."

"Clint! I swear! I never thought they would do anything to the Nesmiths, other than deplete their bank account by half a million. They wouldn't have been hurt by that. They knew the target was being sought in an illegal manner. They weren't all that innocent. I did *not* have any idea they would be hurt. I knew damned well the Littletons and Guila and Fred would end up, one set of them, dead. Big boo-hoo!"

"I agree, none of them were a loss. Anyone like them, someone who goes into a scheme where they kill someone else for money, knows the rules of that game. It's a risk *you* took, along with them. Why do every one of you think you're, somehow, outside the rules? Are you all so damned stupid ... you're just like politicians. The rules apply to others, not you.

"Got news for you, chump! You went into this with your eyes wide open. You put the blinders on, yourself. Now you're playing last hand. You or Elena win – or the house takes the pot. I'm going to see that the house takes the pot. That puts me at the same risk as you and the lovely Elena. I think I'm good enough at the game to beat someone who lets little details slip by them."

Goins was about to cry. "Little details?"

"Lock the place and leave that balcony door unsecured? That's the little detail that could have ended your seat at the game."

Goins thought hard for a few minutes, while Clint sipped the beer. He wasn't worried about the beer, because everyone knew Goins didn't drink beer. He wanted to know more about Elena Sanchez Vargas Menendez.

"Oh. One other little detail you would tend to

miss. Don't eat or drink anything in this apartment. Valdez and Guila did that. I wonder
mightily where the Littletons got the stuff. The
Cuna sure as all hell didn't give any of it to a
gringo, for any price!"

"Cuna? What...?"

"The poison used to knock off Valdez and
Zacharia was made by the Cuna. They don't let it
get out of their hands. It was supposed to look like
the Ngobe did it, but even they can't get the
poison, and wouldn't use it if ... I'll be damned!
The witch!"

"Witch? What's going on! What witch?"

"This is getting weirder and weirder. I think
there's someone else involved, but don't have a
clue as to how."

"Clint, what do I do now? What would you do in
my position?"

"Your sad position, at the moment, is bent over
with your bare ass sticking up to get a big stiff
one. I'd get the hell out of Panama, personally."

"I can go to Medellin ... or Managua!"

"Why bother? That's the same as here."

"I have relatives in Ontario. I can go there. Or
Sydney."

"Sidney might be safe enough. It's become your
problem."

"I have to make some kind of arrangement to

move the, er, funds.”

“In an account that woman and probably a few friends are watching? Really? That would be smart!”

“Let it sit there a month or so, huh?”

“Maybe two years. There’s no way I can get them all.”

“I think I should make it plain that the money will be totally out of, er, anyone else’s reach, if anything happens to me, don’t you?”

“I suppose.”

Goins looked entirely defeated. Clint studied him a little as he got another cold beer from the ‘fridge. He smirked to himself, walked out on the balcony to drink the beer, then went in to say he had to make a few calls, then he’d probably go back to Cusapín. He used the bathroom, looked at the things there, and decided, seeing there were witches and such involved, he would take something for them. He knew there was some, maybe not much, but some, truth to psychic powers.

“You’re pretty good! – but not as good as you think you are!” he mumbled, as he walked toward the bus.

There was still something missing. He changed directions and looked for Vargas’s office. He went in to say he had to speak with her, briefly. He waited ten minutes, until an Indio woman left. A woman in the traditional colors of the Cuna Yala. The secretary said for Clint to go in.

Elena Vargas was a mostly-Indio woman. That explained the poison, when added to that Cuna Yala, leaving.

"I just stopped to ask if the witch woman near the comarca is in this mess – or just you?

"Which comarca? Where?" She didn't turn a hair that Clint knew a lot about the deal. He was probably noted from the start. Maybe she thought she was using him, too.

"Cusapín," Clint replied.

"Olafia? We talk, now and then."

Clint nodded and left, without further comment. He went to the bus. Obilio, a friend who helped him in the past, was there, so Clint asked that he keep an eye on Goins. Notice particularly when he went to the bank or when he pretended to leave. See if he could find where he went.

"Should I stop it when anyone wants to kill him?"

Clint thought a moment. "Only if you don't get hurt doing it."

He caught a bus to David. He wondered if Vargas or Goins would be alive in two days.

Clint called Judi when he was in David at the Pension Costa Rica. She had a few little things that helped – such as that there was some black witch-woman involved, somehow. Her name came up twice. Olafia Smith. Judi knew exactly how to not let a person know she even heard something they said. Rolando, a local semi-thug, had said something about her. Luela had said her boss, a local black woman, who was a sort of witch, herself, had let it slip that something was supposed to be done to protect someone else who she didn't like, but was getting scared of. Olafia Something. She had made Wiliam and Jorge go back to Colon.

Clint had it all, he thought. It was a matter of four sets of schemes backfiring against themselves. The first set was what had happened in Cusapín and in that area. Now this mess Goins was trying to use to manipulate Clint into getting rid of Elena for him. That was ... damn it! It could be just one or two working together!

But Clint had enough with this to finish it, he was sure. "Strike two!" he said, aloud.

Obilio called. Goins was going to Panamá City. He went to the bank and got a long readout and signature on an account ledger. He managed to be waiting for the consultant on the seat by the office door. He heard it all. Goins and the bank manager both spoke English – but, as they did NOT know, so did Obilio.

"They will transfer almost a million dollars to an account in the Banco Global. It will cost Goins more than nine hundred dollars."

"Thanks, Obilio. That tells me a lot."

Clint went to a good meal at Las Brasas, then went to Bohmfalk's. They had the bar and restaurant in Bocas Town when Clint first went there. They sold that place and had just opened the bar and restaurant in David. He then went to Peter's at the Hotel Iris where he chatted with friends. He turned in about ten thirty.

He caught a very early bus, in the morning, to Chiriqui Gande. He managed to leave the Costa Rica by the back entrance, where no one who was watching the place would know. It probably wasn't necessary, but he wouldn't take any chances. It was about 6:45 when he got to Chiriqui Grande.

Clint went to the police station to talk with Oliveros. He knew he would have the morning shift, because it was early when Moises called them about Valdez and company. he came. He knew who the witch woman was and warned Clint that she had a reputation for using poisons that they couldn't trace or prove. He suspected strongly that she was behind the deaths of Valdez and Zacharia.

"I think maybe she's behind a lot of things. All I have to know is who else is involved with her. It's one of two people," Clint explained. "I have to talk to her. I may have enough information that I can get her to slip up. I only need to know a few things.

"I don't think she was directly involved in the poisoning of the Littletons. I have to know, definitely. She might have made the suggestion that led to that part."

Oliveros nodded. He wished Clint luck.

Clint went out to the dock. None of his regular friends were around, this morning. He went back into town to a restaurant and asked how he could get to the village where Olafia Smith was staying. He was told there was a road, not very good, but not too bad, from Rambala. He was directed to it. He could probably walk there in less than an hour. Michael, a friend from Changuinola, was there. He said he'd take him in his truck part of the way, but the road was too bad, after the river.

Clint took him up on that and was taken to where

it only took about twenty minutes to walk the rest of the way. He came into the village to find a pretty young black girl, waiting for him. She said the witch-woman said she had a vision that he would come.

Yeah. And I didn't see that waitress at the restaurant run in to call her when I asked how to find her!

"She is very powerful. She knows what will happen. It happens many times, here. She said to bring Mr. Clint to her house early, because she has much work with the spirits of some people who were murdered in the comarca. They want everyone to know she was not the one who sent the death potion to them.

So she's covering her ass with the locals. She maybe didn't send it, but she damned well knows who did.

Clint walked with the girl to a house that was full of the things mediums and witches always had around. The girl introduced her to a large black woman with dark sunglasses that Clint was surprised she could see through in that darkened house.

"I know you. I know your soul. You are a man, partly good, partly bad. You seek revenge on those who killed the friends of your friend who lives somewhere to the west and near the sea. The people were given a poison that is not from here. It is a poison that none can ever prove. I tell you it was that poison you have suspected by the word of a ... very wise and loyal ... possibly Indio. Name begins with an `N' ... or ... no! `M'. Very surely an `M'!

"I am correct, no?"

"No. They weren't friends. Quite the opposite. It's not revenge I seek, it's truth. Two of those people were innocent. They were brought into this by trickery. I don't like schemes that bring innocent people into them – and I certainly want justice for them. I want to have the people responsible for that caught and prosecuted. I came here to find how deeply involved you are. Elena Vargas hinted that you're very deeply involved."

"Elena Vargas is who?"

"Elena Sanchez Vargas Menendez. Living in Puerto Armuelles."

"The lawyer woman? I spoke with her one time about some maps that were phony. She wanted me to tell some people they were real. That I spoke with the spirits who made them and they are real. She offered me five hundred dollars.

"I would not do that. I do many things that are spoken of as evil. I do not like the Indios, but I am black, and few black people like Indios.

"I understand that the culture is the reason. Our

cultures do not blend, in many parts. I do them no harm, though I am accused of anything that goes wrong on the comarca."

"No. You aren't blamed for anything on the comarcas. They have their own witch women who counter any spells or such. They say you do not send spells there. They know it's cultural conflict. They do say you are much too free with poisons, which is why they suspected you. Moises told them the poison was one that is not available to you. There's a damned good reason no one would believe they used the poison, anyway.

"I wanted to know if you're involved. I'll tell you definitely that you're in danger. They're dangerous people. There's a lot of money involved. That's a bad situation, when people are killed for the money, then someone steals the money from the killer."

She studied Clint for a minute, took off the sunglasses, and said it was a relief to be able to see, for a change.

"I'm from Jamaica, Mon. This is an act that keeps me free, and I can eat regular-like. I make some poisons, but they are only used by my own race. I know there are very evil black people here – more than most other places, except Jamaica and Haiti. I do not feel regret that they use those poisons on each other, so much, Mon. They aren't so messy as a machete or Uzzi.

"I checked with a friend in Santiago on the dead people. Their deaths were ordered by a person now in Puerto Armuelles. Maybe the lawyer-woman. Maybe an Englishman. It is one or the other. It may be both, but I think that is not the way it is."

"So do I. I only have to know who's really behind it, then I'll put an end to it, one way or another.

"I'm – or was – being used. *That*, I resent, more because they assumed I'm stupid than because they tried to use me."

"I do have some very small powers. You will not believe that, but I do. I was always with it from a small child. I can tell much about a person, if I have some very personal item."

Clint grinned and took a plastic envelope from his pocket. He said it was used by the person in question – or not. If she could read anything from it, she would know.

She nodded. She carefully unfolded the envelope to take the razor to touch it to her lips.

"It is the item from a very, very evil person. A man, not from here. He could ... is the Englishman in Puerto Armuelles. He plots and plans evil things. He is in fear for his life. He is causing the death of an evil woman, just now. He feels she has done something ... to kill him. He must be first. She has been the cause of the deaths of others, but from what he did ... or told her ... or something.

"That is all. He has a very dark soul. He has many fears. He wants money, for the money. He has much money, but wants more."

"Was he the one who caused the deaths of the people here?"

"... I ..." She touched the razor to her lip again, for a few seconds. "This may be not total in correctness, but ... it is mixed. He caused the deaths of ... partners? He is angry and afraid, because the first ones ... were not supposed to die, only to ... only to supply money. It is always money, with him.

"The maps! *He* made the maps with fire and ... acid? ... or something."

Clint nodded. He gave her a twenty dollar bill for a consultation fee. She grinned and touched the bill to her lip. She looked surprised.

"You are a good man, in many ways. You are, how do you say? Outraged that the innocent were harmed. I think I like you. Mon! I don't meet too many people who are honest."

"You know something? I think I like you, too! Good fortune!"

Clint left. He headed for Chiriqui Grande. He would have to go to Panamá City. As he had suspected, since meeting with Goins, Goins was behind the whole sick mess – but not behind the deaths of the Nesmiths. He would do something to take Vargas's end of it away. He didn't know how to tag her for the murders of anyone. He had no proof. What a witch said didn't hold one gram of weight in court.

He went on to Bocas Town, got fresh clothes, checked everything at his house, there, and spent an hour over dinner with Judi, Dave and Ben. He told them more-or-less what he'd learned. He was just getting on the water taxi to go to the bus in Almirante when his phone buzzed. It was Obilio.

"Clint? We just got word that Mr. Goins caught the bus for Panamá City in David and was dead in his seat when they arrived at Santiago. No one knows why he died."

"How long ago?" Clint asked.

"I had the call from Jorge just five minutes ago."

Clint talked a couple of minutes. He decided the only difference was that he would go to Puerto Armuelles. He told Obilio to see if Goins ate or drank anything on the bus.

So. Sweet little Elena managed to get some of the poison to him. How? Was he so stupid he took something from his apartment to snack on during the ride?

Obilio called. He said he bought a soda from a

girl when he got on the bus. She stood by the door to the bus, selling sodas and galetas.

"In a box or lata?" Clint asked.

"Box. It has a straw."

That didn't make much sense, but Clint let it pass. Obilio would have an obvious answer.

What the hell! "Why does a straw make a difference?"

"With the straw, it's sealed, if the bus hits a desnivel. A lata is open, and will spill."

Like he thought. Obvious.

So. She injected the drink the same way the drinks for Valdez and Zacharia were injected with the same poison. No doubt there about who was behind that!

How could he prove anything about Vargas? That was going to be one hell of a problem.

Clint thought about how he would handle this mess. He didn't want Vargas to get away with anything. She was the one who had the Nesmiths killed.

Clint got off the bus in David and went to the Costa Rica. Lee had assumed he would be back, because of the way he left, so he went to the same room. He went to La Tipica, which is open 24 hours, to get some shrimp apanada. Delicious. He then went back to the Costa Rica and to bed. In the morning, he went to the bus station and headed for Puerto Armuelles. He stopped in Frontera to talk with some friends there, then went on. When he arrived, he called Obilio and had him meet at Yola's Restauratnt. Clint asked what had happened since the notice that Goins was dead. Obilio said, "Not much. Vargas wasn't going to her office today. She was laying low somewhere. No one knew where she was. She wouldn't answer calls."

Clint sighed. He asked where she lived.

"The big house on the paved road out onto the peninsula. The white one with bricks. She isn't there. Her car is gone."

Clint wrinkled his forehead. "Where was she when Goins left. Her office?"

"No. She had that Indio woman to her office with a girl. They told the girl to deliver something to David at the bus terminal and to wait on the right bus or for someone to come there or something. I wasn't close enough to hear much. They went out, then she took the car and no one saw her since. Goins left about half an hour later. He went to the bank I told you about, then went somewhere in a taxi. I didn't follow, because there was no taxi close."

"Do you know which taxi?"

"Yes. I wrote the number." He took a slip of paper, torn from something from his pocket, and handed it to Clint. Clint talked another couple of minutes, then Obilio left to go to work. Clint stayed in Yola's Restaurant. All the local taxis came by there. Clint saw the taxi he wanted and asked where he had taken the Englishman.

"That Goins person? Just to Emilio's. By the Alba Road."

Clint thanked him.

Where was the car? It would have to be close. He walked around a bit, then took a taxi to drive out the Alba Road, for a short distance. The Mitsubishi was under some trees, a few blocks out. Clint had the taxi wait and went to the car. She was behind the wheel – with a bullet hole between her eyes.

So. Strike three, and you're out! Everybody managed to kill off everybody else. Now and then, things work out pretty well! He wouldn't have to worry about Vargas getting away with anything.

He called the police and explained enough about what had happened for them to be able to close the case as a revenge killing by a person who was now also dead.

Clint headed for David and the bus to Bocas. He would like to be able to relax for a few days.

Maxie, the loan officer for the Banco Nacional de Panamá, called to him when he passed and asked what was to be done with his money. The transfer was cancelled when Mr. Goins died and there were instructions that any and all funds held by Mr. Goins were to be inherited by Clint, if anything happened to him within thirty days. It was more than eight hundred fifty five thousand dollars, altogether. Clint groaned and said he would come back next week and they could transfer it to the new hospital fund. Maxie almost fainted. He said they could build the whole hospital for that!

"Then that's what we'll do!" Clint agreed.

He went on and caught the bus.

Clint walked along the beach with Andres, Moises, and Dave. They watched a large cayuca going along the coast and called their "Oye!" call. Things were peaceful. Dave was going along the beach in the morning to take up his classification studies, again. They'd discussed the murders as much as they would. It was in the past. It didn't really concern the comarca. Life there would go on as always.

"We are going to go to the mountain tomorrow evening for the reading of the signs. Would you care to come along?" Moises asked.

Clint thought about it a few seconds.

"I'll pass."

C. D. Moulton's works are available on most major outlets as printed or e-books. CD writes the CD Grimes, PI, mysteries, the Det. Lt. Nick Storie mysteries, the Clint Faraday mysteries, the Flight of the Maita science fiction series, books on orchid culture and many others of many types. Mystery, adventure, intrigue, science fiction, humor, fantasy, paranormal, mild erotica, and factual.

www.ingramcontent.com/pod-product-compliance
Lightning Source LLC
Chambersburg PA
CBHW051341150726
48000CB00015B/1004